TUPILAQ

By CHRISTOFFER PETERSEN

Published by Aarluuk Press

Copyright © Christoffer Petersen 2017
This edition 2018

Christoffer Petersen has asserted his right under the Copyright, Designs and Patents Act 1988 to be identified as the author of this work.

This book is a work of fiction. The names, characters, places and incidents are products of the writer's imagination or have been used fictitiously and are not to be construed as real. Any resemblance to persons, living or dead, actual events or organisations is entirely coincidental.

All rights reserved. No part of this publication may be reproduced, stored in a retrieval system, or transmitted, in any form or by any means, without the prior permission in writing of the publisher, nor be otherwise circulated in any form of binding or cover other than that in which it is published and without a similar condition including this condition being imposed on the subsequent purchaser.

ISBN: 978-1-980429-29-6

www.christoffer-petersen.com

And here [Nukúnguasik] came upon the middle one of many brothers, busy with something or other down in a hollow, and whispering all the time. So he crawled stealthily towards him, and when he had come closer, he heard him whispering these words:

"You are to bite Nukúnguasik to death; you are to bite Nukúnguasik to death."

And then it was clear that he was making a Tupilak, and stood there now telling it what to do. But suddenly Nukúnguasik slapped him on the side and said: "But where is this Nukúnguasik?"

And the man was so frightened at this that he fell down dead.

Excerpt from
NUKÚNGUASIK, WHO ESCAPED FROM THE TUPILAK
from
ESKIMO FOLK-TALES
Collected by
KNUD RASMUSSEN (1872-1907)

Tupilaq

CHRISTOFFER PETERSEN

PART 1

I watched the mother weep as she climbed into the helicopter, and during the short flight from the airport at Kulusuk to the helipad in Tasiilaq. Her children clutched at her hands, one on either side, and I felt some pity at their struggle to console their mother. Surely, some great tragedy had struck this east Greenland family, and the journalist in me was curious. Not enough to intrude, or even offer my sympathies – I simply didn't have the language for it. No, I entertained thoughts of a more mercenary nature, encouraged as they were by a looming deadline, and nothing of interest to report on the horizon. It was my rent and not a streak of compassion that kept me within a few metres of the grief-stricken family on landing in Tasiilaq. I followed them into the heliport terminal – a modest size building with a single hangar on the side that could squeeze in a Bell 212 helicopter, or something of a similar size. But it was in the waiting lounge, furnished as it was with plastic chairs and Formica-surfaced tables, that I felt a sudden lift in my fortunes when I saw Constable David Maratse leaning against the wall by the door, studying the new arrivals. He wore a wool hat which surprised me, as it seemed too early for him, winter was only just starting to establish a foothold on the summits of the mountains.

I waved and he acknowledged me with a nod, before turning his attention to the family, and the weeping mother in particular. I watched him observe each of them, tilting his head as he looked at the smallest of the children, a girl, perhaps five years old, with long black hair that reached awkwardly to her bottom. It was cut at an odd angle, and I wondered if her sister, a few years older, had anything to do with it. Maratse picked up the mother's bag and the smallest of the girls. He caught my eye and nodded at the door.

"Do you want a lift?"

"Yes," I said, and shouldered my backpack. I held my laptop bag by the handle, and followed Maratse and the family out of the door. His car, the dark blue police Toyota, was parked with the engine running, on the road beside the heliport. The girl in Maratse's arms fiddled with the collar of his jacket as he opened the boot and dumped the mother's bag inside. He waited for me to throw my backpack inside before closing the boot and helping the small girl into the passenger seat. Maratse nodded for me to sit up front.

The mother said nothing on the drive into town. Maratse looked at her several times as she wiped at her tears, before pulling over onto a patch of gravel by the side of the road. He turned in his seat and looked at her. I fiddled with the handle of my laptop bag. The girls said nothing and the only sound louder than the rumble of the Toyota's engine was the occasional sniffle from the mother.

I had grown accustomed to Greenlandic silences. More to the point, I had learned when to be quiet, such as when eating a meal. Greenlanders enjoyed their food, and, depending on their exposure to Danes and Europeans, they ate in silence, sharing but a few words until the meal was over, before relaxing on the sofa with a coffee or something stronger. Greenlanders were quiet at other times too, and my previous adventure with Maratse had taught me that the Constable was particular with his vocabulary, and not wont to long discussions. His silence was nothing new, but I became increasingly curious about the situation.

Maratse spoke, and the mother answered with a nod, and a brief acknowledgment in east Greenlandic. A grunt from Maratse brought a smile to my face as I remembered similar exchanges when we were searching for a murderer by the name of Aqqalunnguaq in the fjord and mountains surrounding Ittoqqortoormiit, a few hundred kilometres north of Tasiilaq. Aqqalunnguaq killed his brother in a bar, and I wondered, just for a second, if this family was reacting to something equally tragic. Life in Greenland was riddled with tragedy. As if the environment was not harsh enough, the social aspects of life on the east coast, added another dimension, something that my connection with Maratse allowed me access to, often resulting in articles that pleased the editors for whom I toiled. The sound of Maratse's voice, actual words, startled me.

"There should be three," he said, in Danish.

"Three?"

"Children." Maratse dipped his head towards the backseat. "There's only two."

"I'm not sure I understand," I said. "Has something happened?" I imagined the loss of a child, and the level of grief that would evoke. It was not lost on me, but I realised I did not have all the details as yet, and needed more information. I waited as Maratse asked a few more questions. The mother answered. Maratse sighed and pulled his mobile from his pocket.

Whatever the mother had said seemed to be linked to the widening of her daughters' eyes as they listened to Maratse speak on the mobile. I understood why as he spoke to his Danish-speaking partner.

"*Iji*, yes, her son. Nine years old. He has taken a boat, and gone to visit his father." Maratse glanced at me, and said, "In Tiniteqilaaq. Yes, a long way." Maratse ended the call, said something to the mother, and then repeated it for me. "My partner is coming to pick up the family."

"He's coming here?"

"*Iji.*"

"And her son is missing?"

"He's gone to visit his father."

"By himself?"

Maratse nodded, and said, "She has tried to call the father, but he has not answered."

"How long has the boy been gone?" I waited as Maratse turned to ask the mother.

"Two days," he said, and then, "His name is Nakinngi."

Nakinngi. I tested the name on my tongue, resisting the urge to write it down in my notepad. Maratse noticed the twitch of my hands, opened the driver door, and gestured for me to join him outside. There was a bite in the wind, and a quick look at the mountains showed winter creeping down towards the town. I folded my arms across my chest, as Maratse lit a cigarette and rolled it into the gap between his teeth. He stuffed his hands in his jacket pockets and smoked.

We had been here before, he and I, on the cusp of an adventure. Admittedly, he was doing his job, but the idea of an imminent search was something that appealed to me, and would certainly qualify as an interesting article that I could sell. I decided to test the waters.

"What are you doing in Tasiilaq?" I asked.

"A colleague is on holiday. I am covering his shifts." Maratse looked at me through the cloud of smoke he puffed out of his lungs. His hands were firmly in his pockets.

"Are you going to search for the boy?"

Maratse nodded, and said, "As soon as the Dane gets here."

"The Dane?"

"Another colleague, also temporary."

I turned at the sound of an approaching vehicle, and saw the familiar dark blue of Tasiilaq's second police Toyota, as it slowed to a stop in front of us. The mother and her girls got out of Maratse's car, collected their things, and walked the short distance to the other car. Maratse nodded at his colleague, and flicked the butt of his cigarette into the gravel by the side of the road.

"You'll take them home?" he asked.

"To the station first. I'll get a statement." The police officer glanced at me, and then said, "When will you leave?"

"Now," Maratse said. "I'm taking him with me," he said, and pointed at me.

"Why?"

"Ballast," Maratse said, and grinned. I was still processing the idea of getting into a small fibreglass dinghy and sailing across the fjord to what I knew was a tiny settlement with just a handful of people living there. But, somehow, Maratse's practical application of my body weight reassured me, and I worked hard to control the grin on my face.

"You're sure you don't want me to go?" the

police officer asked. "You were ready to call in sick this morning."

"The fresh air will help," Maratse said. "And, you don't know the way."

"True," the man nodded. "Just take plenty of gear and food."

"Coffee and cigarettes." Maratse laughed.

"All right then. I'll take the family back to the station. Let me know when you leave."

I watched as they shook hands and then climbed back into the passenger seat when Maratse nodded that it was time to go. The mother, I noticed, was still crying. She held her girls on the back seat. I watched them until we pulled away.

Greenland is a country with a very simple, if expensive, travel network. There are no roads connecting the towns, villages, and settlements. To get from one place to another, one flew, usually in a de Havilland Dash 7 with four engines, or the newer and faster Dash 8 with two. Gravel airstrips connected the smaller towns with the larger asphalt runways of Ilulissat, Qaqortoq, and Maniitsoq, and the capital of Nuuk. But travel beyond the small airports usually required a connecting flight with a helicopter, and sometimes a boat. To get to Tiniteqilaaq, without chartering a special flight, would mean taking a small boat. I experienced a twinge of my stomach muscles when Maratse parked beside the boat he said we would take to find the boy.

"Why can't we just call?" I asked, as I got out of the car and looked at the small dinghy bobbing in the water in the wake of a fishing cutter.

"The mother said she had tried."

"Can't we try again?" I said, and studied the

dinghy. The water in the bottom of the boat looked to be as deep as my fist. The blood stains from a recent hunting trip hid patches of rust to all but the most observant sailor, and in that moment, I was most observant.

"You don't have to come," Maratse said, as he opened the Toyota's boot.

"No, I want to," I said, whispering to myself that actually, "I needed to." But faced with the reality of a long cold trip at sea on the east coast of Greenland, I was overcome by a sudden urge for self preservation. "Whose boat is this?"

"Mine," said Maratse. He smiled as he walked to the boat, leaned over the side, and pulled an insulated set of overalls from a plastic chest in front of the thwart seat in the centre. He tossed the overalls onto the rocks and pulled out another. "Yours," he said, as he handed me a set of overalls. The material was cold and greasy. It reminded me of a skin, flensed from a sea creature. It smelled of fish, blood, and tobacco. I carried it to the boot, draping it over the bumper, as I pulled several layers, a fleece jacket, hat and gloves from my backpack. Maratse fished a pair of socks from the pockets of his overalls and pressed them into my hands. "For the boots," he said, as I wrinkled my nose. The socks were damp, but I realised I wouldn't care, just as soon as I couldn't smell them.

We dressed and stowed the rest of our gear in the boot of the Toyota. I stuffed my notepad and pencils in the chest pocket of my overalls, and slid my laptop bag alongside my backpack.

"I have biscuits and cigarettes in the boat," Maratse said, with a gesture at the dinghy. He removed his utility belt, pistol and his police jacket, before zipping his overalls all the way to the lip of the collar. Maratse buckled his pistol around his waist, and put his jacket on again. I noticed a brief wave of calm flow over him once he had his jacket on, as if it was an essential layer of clothing, a piece of his armour, something that made him whole. It was, I realised, only slightly cleaner than the overalls.

I finished dressing and pulled the damp socks over my own, as Maratse handed me a pair of black rubber boots with orange caps. He waited for me to nod that I was ready, and then closed and locked the police car.

"Shall we go?" he asked.

The salt in the air merged with a cold breath from a large iceberg just off the shore, and pricked at the hairs inside my nose. I pulled on my gloves and nodded.

"I'm ready," I said.

Maratse pointed at the lines secured to a rusted chain looped around a rock, and we prepared to cast off.

PART 2

There is a trick to sailing in small open boats in Greenland. If one imagines extreme cold and discomfort before the journey begins, then one is not disappointed. The very fact that it is exactly as one predicted provides one with a sense of satisfaction and reassurance that some things are just meant to be. There is an old adage that there is no such thing as bad weather, just bad clothes, but I would have to disagree. The cold air coming off the ice sheet and the icebergs, plus the wind, and, not least, the temperature of the water, these things combined strip away any comfort one might have in the layers one has put on. Of course, it could also be the fact that I am Danish, European, and simply not built for these waters. Maratse seemed unaffected by the cold, and he had that look in his eye, as he smoked, of utter contentment, a sense of peace that all was as it should be. I tried, I really did, to look around me, to *see* the beauty of the land and the sea, and I would have – I know I would have – had I not been utterly miserable, as the cold seeped through the very stitches of each of my many layers, and gnawed at my bones. Maratse steered the boat with naked hands on the tiller. He did, however, wear the wool hat still, and it seemed out of character.

He slowed as we approached Tiniteqilaaq, a tiny settlement of roughly seventy residents, whose primary means of existence came from the sea and the land. I looked at the houses as Maratse idled the motor and we drifted towards the shore. The walls of each house were wind-bitten, the roofs tacked, tarred, and patched, and the spaces between each house crowded with hunting and fishing paraphernalia, an Arctic museum curator's dream. To my untrained eye, everything looked old, beaten by the weather, beaten by man, beaten by time. Wood was grey and husky, metal orange with rust, and the fur of the dogs was matted with the grime of summer. But soon it would be winter, and for all its bluster, it would be easier. Interminably hard, but easier all the same, as everything slowed and froze, preserved for the remainder of the year.

Maratse bumped the dinghy against the rocks, waited for me to scramble over the side, and threw me a line to secure our arrival. For lack of anything better, I tied Maratse's dinghy to the hull of another dinghy just a few metres further up the beach. We were at once surrounded by sledge dog puppies and children, who in turn attracted the slow amble of two fishermen.

"Taratsi?" Maratse said, and it took me a moment to realise it was the name of the father. The fishermen pointed towards a house, and I followed Maratse to the door. He knocked and we entered.

The inside of Taratsi's house was lit with the late sun of early winter, filtered as it was though a smear of salt grime on the windows. Taratsi sat at a small table beside the wood stove. He was reading a newspaper with yellowed edges, his arm resting on an open book. I was surprised, even more so when I realised the book was a dictionary, and the paper was open at the crossword puzzle. Several lines had been solved already, in several styles of handwriting and colours of ink. A community effort, perhaps?

Maratse knocked on the door frame, as he entered the kitchen. Taratsi looked up and they exchanged a few words and a smile when Maratse pointed at me and said something that made them both laugh. They talked for a few minutes before Maratse asked about Nakinngi.

"Nakinngi?" the man said, and I recognised the look of a parent who suddenly noticed the police uniform Maratse wore. Taratsi started to speak, and Maratse whispered the translation.

"He hasn't seen him for over two months. The last time was in the summer, in Tasiilaq, when he and the mother met in court to discuss custody. They are not married." Maratse paused to listen, as Taratsi continued.

I studied the face of the man, as the lines and wrinkles ingrained by the long polar summer furrowed with a sense of profound sadness, as soon as he realised that his son was missing, perhaps drowned.

"I didn't say that," Maratse said, "but he is right to think it."

"You think the boy is drowned?" I asked.

Maratse shrugged, and said, "Maybe." He kicked off his boots and stepped into the kitchen, leaning up against the counter as Taratsi began to talk about his son. Maratse, I noticed, seemed pale all of a sudden. The light in his eyes that shone so brightly in the fjord was dulled. He shook his head when I caught his eye, and said, "I'm okay."

"You're sure?"

"*Iiji.*" Maratse looked at Taratsi, waited for him to stop talking, and then said something that seemed to give the father hope. He looked at me and said, "I told him we would search for his son. I told him that's why you were here – two pairs of eyes."

"Right," I said, and smiled at the father.

"There's a problem," Maratse said.

"Oh?"

"He has no idea where he might have gone."

The father looked at me, his lips flat, almost quivering, as he said, "I don't know."

Maratse said a few more words, and then nodded to me that we were leaving. He shook Taratsi's hand, picked up his boots, and leaned against the door as he pulled one and then the other onto his feet. The fresh air seemed to give Maratse a boost. He smoked as we wandered back to the dinghy.

"There's a lot of sea," he said, as we stood at the water's edge. He waved a hand at the fjord, and said, "Even with a helicopter, I'm not sure where we should begin."

"Around the island?" I said. "To start with."

"The boy is dead," Maratse said. "We can sail for a few hours, maybe stay here tonight, and search again tomorrow, on our way back to town."

I said nothing as Maratse finished his cigarette. The surface of the fjord reflected the grey of the clouds above. It was easier to see the icebergs on an overcast day such as this, but little else. Whatever secrets the fjord may have would remain hidden, lost unless by chance one were to sail into whatever it was one was looking for. A child's body, if not below the surface already, was but a tiny drop in a vast obsidian sea.

Maratse tugged his mobile from his jacket pocket and called the police station in Tasiilaq. He paced as he talked, dogged as he was by a string of curious puppies, attached to the toes of his boots with an invisible length of elastic. They were amusing, lifting the sadness of the moment with their antics. I was so engrossed I did not hear the man's approach, and his voice startled me, not least because he spoke in Danish.

"I will sell you one or all of them," the man said.

"The puppies?" I said, as I turned to look at him.

"Yes, the puppies. Will you buy them?"

"No. I don't need any puppies."

"Good, because they are not mine." The man grinned, and I noticed he had fewer teeth than Maratse. Dentists, I remembered, were a luxury in Greenland, travelling as they did in roving bands of teeth-pullers up and down the coast. This man was different too in that his shock of hair was grey, and his skin, paler than the Greenlanders I had met on the east coast, was pitted and pocked with what looked like acne scars. He was not, I realised, a handsome man, and neither was he particularly endearing, bent as he was on selling me something. "Like this boat," he said, and pointed at Maratse's dinghy.

"I came on that boat," I said.

"Of course," he said. His head bobbed as he laughed. "But is it yours?"

"No. It's his." I pointed at Maratse.

"Then you do not have a boat?"

"No." I glanced at Maratse, anxious that he might intervene.

"Ah, then you need a boat. Good," the man said. "I will find a boat for you."

"Hey," I said, "just a minute. I don't want to buy anything."

"No?"

"No."

"That is a pity." If the man had been a child, then

the expression on his face might have been fitting. As it was, he looked ridiculous, pouting dark lips between the scars on a grey face.

"Hello Ivik," Maratse said, as he slipped his mobile in his pocket. He shook the man's hand, and introduced me.

"You have an assistant."

"Sort of," Maratse said. He nodded at his dinghy and began untying the knot I had looped through the other boat. "We have to be going."

"Already?"

"*Iji.*" Maratse pointed up at the sky, and said, "Not much light left."

"You are looking for the boy?"

"You know about that?" I said.

"I know lots of things."

Maratse sighed and let go of the rope. "Not now, Ivik." He looked at me, and said, "Ivik thinks he is a wise man."

"I am a shaman," he said, and plucked at my sleeve. "I know lots of things."

"Really?" Despite the look on Maratse's face I was intrigued.

"We have to go," Maratse said. He gestured for me to help him push the dinghy off the rocks and into the water.

"But where will you go?" Ivik said. "You don't know where to begin. I can help you."

"*Eeqqi,*" Maratse said. "We don't want your magic."

"Magic?" The word hung between us for a moment, and the shaman grabbed at it, teasing it into something that he could sell, if not to Maratse, then to his assistant.

"Yes, magic," he said. "If you will find the boy, then you must go where I tell you. But it is not safe," he said. "You will need my magic to protect you."

"Come on," Maratse said with a light slap on my arm. "We have to go."

"But if he can help us?"

Maratse gave me a look, and had I been less intrigued by the shaman, and less motivated by the need for a story to sell to my editor, I might have blanched. As it was, I blundered on.

"You said it," I whispered, "the boy is dead. We don't know where to begin to look. If this is for show, then what do we have to lose?"

"I won't pay him for information."

"You won't," I said. "It's for magic, and I will pay him."

"There is a mountain in the fjord," Ivik said, and pointed to the north and a knuckle west of Tiniteqilaaq. "But it is very dangerous. You will need protection."

"What kind of protection?" I asked, ignoring Maratse's snort, as he lit another cigarette.

"From the *erqigdlit*."

"What?"

"A beast. The lower body, the back legs, and the tail is that of a wolf, but the body is human. The face is striking, the females beautiful, and naked," Ivik said, his eyes shining. They live where the rock meets the ice, and they are very dangerous. It is there you will find the boy."

Maratse snorted again, and I shushed him, and said, "You said something about protection?"

"Yes," Ivik said. "You will need something strong and powerful, potent," he said. "But it will not be cheap."

"What won't be cheap? What are you going to make?"

Ivik smiled, and said, "I will make you a tupilaq."

"Like the ones in the tourist shops?" I said, with a look at Maratse.

"No, no," Ivik said. "I will make you a *tupilaq*, it is different, very different. It will protect you, maybe even save your life."

Maratse shrugged when I looked at him. "We have to be in Tasiilaq tomorrow night," he said, and pointed at the shaman. "Pay the man, and we can begin."

PART 3

I had expected something different. Perhaps it was the promise of magic, or the fact that Maratse had called Ivik a shaman, but I was slightly disappointed when we followed Ivik into his house. It was cramped, like the other houses in Tiniteqilaaq, but the windows were clean, there were decorative plates hung on the walls, a painting on the far wall of the lounge. Where I had expected to see husks of birds, dice crudely carved from whale bones, feathers, jars of strange viscous liquids, there was only order, cleanliness, no oddity to speak of. Even Ivik seemed to shrug off his strangeness like a cloak he left on a hook at the door. It all seemed so normal, for lack of a better word. I was tempted to leave my notebook in my pocket as I unzipped my overalls and stepped out of them and my boots, but the look on Maratse's face gave me pause. The resolute police constable that I had come to admire seemed positively ill at ease. He lingered at the door, took his time to remove his jacket, to unbuckle his belt, and to remove his overalls. The way he looked at the walls, it was as if he could see through the mirage of bland orderliness. He, at least, could see the supernatural that I hankered after, and I was envious, almost annoyed at the fact. And then the writer in me took over, and I began to observe.

On closer inspection, as Ivik boiled water for tea, I noticed that the decorative plates were not dusted but washed, replaced, perhaps, after each meal. The painting on the wall in the lounge shone, as if it was still wet, and the sills of the windows were burned with the shadows of things that had been on display, during the long polar summer, only to have been removed, used, or hidden. There was a trace of something in the air, a tang with the prick of a fibre of glass, slimmer than a needle. I caught it in my nose if I moved my head too quickly, as I did, when Ivik handed me a glass of tea. I had not heard him approach. Maratse sat at the table in the kitchen, watching me through the open doorway, as Ivik gestured for me to sit on the coach. This was my show, I realised, as Maratse sipped his tea from afar, his gaze at once drawn to my conversation with the shaman, and the front door.

"How is your tea?" Ivik said.

"It's fine. Thank you."

"And you are comfortable?"

"Yes," I said, and glanced at Maratse.

"Don't mind the Constable, he is content to listen. But you are the customer. I am making the tupilaq for you."

"Will it protect us both?"

"Of course, provided I place a little something of each of you inside it." Ivik grinned, and said, "A hair will do."

I sipped at the sweet black tea as Ivik opened a cupboard and pulled out several plastic tubs with lids. The faded lettering and logos on the sides suggested they might once have contained ice cream, but now… I wrinkled my nose at the smell as Ivik opened each box. Here were the husks of birds, the beaks, the nibs, bones with pliable black flesh, lengths of sinew, lengths of seaweed, lengths of hair – too long to be animal. The shaman's boxes were both rich and ripe. They were fascinating.

"You may make notes," Ivik said, "but

photographs will cost you more."

"How much more?" I asked, only to realise I had left my camera in my backpack.

"One hundred Danish kroner, per photo." Ivik sat on a wooden chair opposite me, and laid each box on the coffee table in front of him. He selected various bones, favouring those with a layer of black flesh through which he thread a length of sinew with a bone needle. I rested my notepad on my knee, but did not write a single word, as I watched Ivik stitch a crude figure in the shape of a man. He talked as he worked, describing the *erqigdlit*, praising them, flattering them, fooling them, I realised, blinding them to the arrival of two men searching for a boy lost on the border between rock and ice, somewhere high on a mountainside, in the fjord, at the beginning of winter.

The tupilaq took form, and I swear, to this day, and until the end of my days, that it moved, a twitch at the very least. Ivik looked up, and I realised I might have gasped. He winked and continued to work, flattering the *erqigdlit* once again for their almond-shaped faces, soft caramel skin, long black hair, and sharp, bright, white teeth. He was particularly enamoured with their hands, and he told them so, wondering at how soft they were when one considered that they used them like paws to bound across the rocks. He praised the time they took to groom, recognised that it was important, not something to be shucked or ignored. The bush of their tails would keep them warm this winter, he said, and suggested that it would not be so, were it not for the time they spent caring for them.

"Look after your body," he said to me, "and your

body will look after you." Ivik held the tupilaq up to the light, turned it within his fingers, and tied small knots at the end of each sinew. The bones rattled in a skeleton that fit in the palm of his hand – the hand of the shaman.

"Is it finished?" I asked. "Is that magic?"

"Magic?"

"For protection?"

"No, not yet," Ivik said. "I need something from you."

"A hair?" I said, and plucked one from my head.

"Pubic is best," he said, and grinned. "It is stronger."

"I see."

"I will look away."

Ivik laid the tupilaq on the table, and went into the kitchen. He talked with Maratse as I stuffed my hand down my trousers and tugged a hair from my crotch.

"What I do for a story?" I whispered to myself, and then cringed, as I remembered that the story was ultimately about a boy, and the search for his dead body. I placed the hair next to the tupilaq, careful not to touch it. It had no head to speak of, or rather, the body was elongated, with no visible neck. The stomach, as I chose to call the cavity in the centre of the torso, was empty.

"Thank you," Ivik said, as he returned. He placed a black hair beside mine, one of Maratse's, I imagined, plucked simply from the wool hat he wore on his head. Ivik stuffed both hairs inside the tupilaq's stomach, together with a thumb-sized fluff of fibre that could have been animal, or perhaps just a wisp of frayed plastic twine. "I need to charge it," he said, and picked up the tupilaq.

"Do what?"

"Charge it with energy."

"Don't ask him," Maratse said, as he appeared at the door. He looked pale again, and I thought we had better get him outside. He showed me the packet of cigarettes in his hand, and nodded at the door. I followed him to the steps of Ivik's house, and we sat on the top step, wriggling our toes inside thick wool socks as Maratse smoked.

"You don't believe in magic?" I asked.

"I don't like it," he said.

"Why?"

"It can't be explained."

I remembered that he read science fiction books, and teased him about it.

"You think science fiction is fantasy, but it is based on fact," he said.

"Not all of it. Some of it is pure supposition."

"But it could happen," he said. "One day."

"But magic happens now, every day," I said, and gestured at the fjord. "How do you explain wind?"

"Temperature."

"But can you see it?"

Maratse blew out a cloud of smoke and poked at it with the tip of his cigarette.

"All right, how about time. Can you see that?"

"*Iji*," he said, and picked at a splinter of grey wood on the steps. "But magic," he said, and grasped at the air in front of my face, "is nothing." He opened his palm and turned it in front of me.

I considered a suitable response, but Ivik interrupted my thoughts, as he stepped out of the house onto the short deck between the door and the steps.

"You're finished?"

"Yes," he said, and presented me with a dirty white cloth bound with thick plastic line, the kind used to make fishing nets. Ivik held onto the package as I took it, and said. "Five hundred kroner."

"Okay," I said and tugged my wallet out of my pocket. Maratse shook his head and lit another cigarette.

"How do we know if it is working?" I asked, as I paid Ivik and took the package; it reeked between my fingers.

"You will know when you meet the *erqigdlit*."

"They exist? I thought that was just a story."

"If you did not believe me, why did you pay for the tupilaq?" Ivik stuffed the five hundred kroner note in his pocket and went back inside his house.

"We should be going," Maratse said, and stood up. He flicked the butt of his cigarette into the tough grasses growing beneath the steps.

"Do you know where?"

"Ivik showed me on the map." Maratse opened the door and handed me my boots and overalls. He grabbed his gear and we dressed on the deck. Maratse's gaze drifted a couple of times to the cloth-bound effigy, and I wondered just how much fiction he could accept with his science. I decided not to mention it. I picked up the tupilaq and followed Maratse to the boat, stopping once to wave at the window of the shaman's house, but he was nowhere to be seen.

The children and the puppies watched as we launched Maratse's dinghy, and climbed aboard. The motor started on the second tug of the handle, and

Maratse steered us away from the settlement and into the fjord. The hull bumped against small clumps of ice, and I felt the familiar chill press its way through my clothes and against my skin as it sought out my blood and bones. I regretted, for a moment, not asking the shaman to make me a tupilaq to protect me from the cold, but for five hundred kroner I could have bought a new fleece.

Maratse slowed at the opening of a deep northern bay of the fjord circling the island of Ammassalik, and I sat up to scan the water over the dinghy's bow. Binoculars, that we did not have, would have been useful, but I still felt a rush of excitement as I spotted the hull of a small white dinghy in the distance. It was on the northern coast of the fjord, and I directed Maratse towards it.

"It looks old," he said, as we slowed to within ten metres of the rocks. "Look, the hull is broken. This is not Nakinngi's boat."

"But we should look," I said, and glanced up at the mountainside. I felt a second rush of excitement at the sight of a clear boundary between the rock and the layer of ice above it. Maratse guided the dinghy onto the shallow beach beside the hull of the fibreglass boat, and I leaped over the side with the line, splashing through the frigid water to tie Maratse's boat to the thick exposed roots of a polar birch, stunted as it was by too many winters. Maratse cut the motor and joined me on the beach.

He inspected the boat, and any elation I might have felt at finding it, and seeing the physical incarnation of Ivik's mythical story, drained from my body. The boat was surely too old to be Nakinngi's. I almost said as much. But then Maratse leaned over the broken hull, pressed his hand into a gap beneath the seat at the rear of the dinghy, and pulled out a backpack with the familiar logo of a Danish toy manufacturer.

"This doesn't belong to a hunter," Maratse said, and looked up at the mountainside. He inspected the insides of the backpack, found Nakinngi's name stencilled on the inside, and showed it to me.

"This is good," I said.

"*Iiji*," Maratse said and dumped the rucksack in his dinghy. He tightened his belt and pointed up the slope. "Come on," he said. "I want to be back before it gets dark."

PART 4

We left the backpack in Maratse's boat and started to climb up the mountainside, following a path of sorts, too narrow to be made by human feet, too wide to be a coincidence. Black lichen blistered on the rocks on either side, highlighted in between with a patch of stubborn snow, leached of moisture and gravely to the touch. There was more snow above us, larger patches in the shadow of boulders and rocky outcrops. I stopped to examine one just off the path as Maratse caught up. It was unusual for him to be so slow. I was concerned, not least by the fact that he had yet to light a cigarette since we arrived with the boat. He wiped his brow as he stopped next to the patch of snow, tugged his hat down to his ears and caught his breath.

"You're not well."

"I'm fine."

"We should have stayed in Tasiilaq."

"And who would look for the boy?"

He was right, I suppose. But then he also believed the boy to be drowned, until we found the backpack. That's why he was forcing himself up the mountain.

Maratse studied the patch of old snow and pointed at the indentations in the centre. A closer inspection revealed tufts of fur and dirt caught between the pea-sized clumps of snow.

"Foxes," Maratse said. "They lie here in the summer to escape the mosquitoes."

The snow crunched beneath my boots as I walked around the foxes' resting area. The hollows seemed larger than I imagined a fox would need, and my mind wandered to the idea of the shaman's *erqigdlit*. Did they come this far down the mountain? I caught myself, and laughed at how much I wanted such a beast to exist.

"What's so funny?" Maratse asked.

"*Erqigdlit*," I said, "they could have rested here."

"You mustn't believe everything Ivik says."

"No?" I said and walked back to the path. "Then why did you let me pay him for a tupilaq?"

Maratse shrugged. "You wanted a story. He needs money."

"But you stayed in the kitchen while he made it."

"I've seen it before."

"Really?" I looked Maratse in the eye, and said, "I thought you were uncomfortable. Frightened, perhaps?"

"Hmm," he grunted and nodded at the ice above us. "We should get going. I don't want to spend the night here."

"All right," I said and followed Maratse up the path.

The air cooled the higher we climbed, but the weather remained calm with grey clouds, heavy with snow. The east coast was notorious for heavy snowfall. I remembered hearing of children sitting on the streetlamps in the winter, and tunnels dug through the snow to connect the houses to the roads, although I had yet to experience it. Such thoughts occupied me as I overtook Maratse and climbed on ahead, stopping once in a while to look back, to enjoy the view, and to wait for the policeman as he toiled up the path.

"He really is sick," I whispered to myself, as he approached. I looked over my shoulder at the lower boundary of the ice, perhaps one hundred metres higher. Looking back down the path, I could just see the boats, Maratse's dinghy and the broken hull of Nakinngi's boat. The fjord was still, with only a hint of wind tickling the surface of the water. We could at least have a quick look at the ice above us, and sail back in the dark. It wouldn't be my first time, and it was second-nature to Maratse. "But he is sick."

"I am fine. We keep going," he said, as he caught up. "And then we turn back."

"To the ice?"

"*Iiji.*"

Maratse patted his breast pocket and my concerns lifted in the moment I thought he was going to light a cigarette, but he lowered his hand again and continued up the path.

It took another thirty minutes to reach the ice. Even I found the going tough as the path disappeared and the incline of the slope increased. The temperature dropped several degrees as the air sank from the summit and slipped over the surface of the ice. There was nothing gravely or desiccated about the ice in front of us. The lower edge was raised above the rocks, and water oozed from beneath it, gushing into streams of grey silt that continued down the mountain to the fjord. The sound of the water was at once calming and cacophonous. We had to raise our voices to talk.

"Where do we look?" I asked.

Maratse sighed, as he looked from left to right. He pointed at a smoother stretch with a large overhanging boulder, and said, "If he is here, that might be a good place to shelter."

"Beneath the boulder?"

Maratse nodded, and said, "There might be a small cave." He started walking parallel to the ice towards the boulder, and I followed, happy to let him lead.

There was no path, and we picked our way as best we could between the rocks and boulders, slipping occasionally on patches of scree and splashing though the melt water. I wondered if the temperature was higher beneath the ice, and how cold it should be for the streams to freeze and stall on the slopes of the mountain. Everything stopped in the winter. The icebergs froze into place in the fjord, the glaciers slowed their crawl to a slumber, and the surface of the water, wind and temperature depending, turned to ice. Only two things moved in the winter, the wind above and the tide below. Everything else stopped, as did Maratse just in front of me. I bumped into his shoulder and he pointed at the boulder ahead of us.

"See the opening?"

"Yes."

"A cave," he said, and walked on, his pace quickening despite the slow onset of his fever.

The cave was more of an overhang, a large space beneath the boulder, walled as it was on either side with great molars of rock. Maratse wiped his brow and squeezed between them and disappeared from view. I called out and he grunted that I should follow him.

I could feel the rock as it cooled my fingers inside my gloves. My overalls scratched on the sides, as I squeezed my way into the cave and found Maratse lying on his side. In the gloom of the cave, I had to blink to see if his eyes were open. The floor was littered in one corner with the husk of a raven, its bones picked clean but for a few feathers on the wing. I sat down and stared at the carcass, at once disappointed that we had not found a blanket, or a single item of clothing, a water bottle even. There was nothing to suggest that Nakinngi had been here.

"Just a cave," Maratse said. He rested his head on a smooth rock, and closed his eyes.

"If Nakinngi even came here," I said, "what was he doing?"

"Hunting," Maratse said. There was a touch of phlegm in his words, and he turned to one side to spit.

"Why? He is just a boy."

"He is a Greenlander. He is eleven. I went on my first hunt with my dogs when I was nine."

"Really? Nine?"

"*Iji.*"

"What did you hunt?"

Maratse chuckled for a moment, coughed to clear his throat, and said, "Nothing." He turned his head and opened his eyes to look at me. "My dogs ran off. I had to walk home."

"How far?"

"One kilometre." Maratse chuckled at the memory.

"Nakinngi came a lot further."

"*Iji.*"

"But you think he is dead."

"Maybe the boat hit some ice. It might have washed onto that beach."

"With his backpack caught beneath the seat," I said. "Yes, that makes sense." I looked at Maratse and said, "I suppose we should go back."

"Hmm," he said. "Five minutes."

"All right," I said. "I will have a look around outside."

"Hmm."

I waited, but Maratse said nothing more. I crawled between the rocks and stepped out from beneath the boulder, suddenly aware of the wind, and how sheltered it was inside the cave.

I thought of Maratse's childhood, and how very different it was from my own. While I was playing video games on my uncle's Atari system, Maratse was harnessing a team of dogs to a sledge and hunting. I drank a litre of cola each weekend, and visited the Burger King with friends. I imagined Maratse, at a similar age, tugging soft seal meat off the bone with his teeth, and drinking cartons of juice from the store through a straw. But we were here now, together, and, as I scanned the boundary between the rock and the ice, I began to appreciate that no matter how different our upbringing, the environment brought us together – the rocks, the ice, and the wind.

The wind.

There was something on the wind, a sound of some description. If we had been in town, or even in a small settlement, I might have a hundred reasons for such a sound. The wind teasing at a loose flap of tarpaulin stretched over a hunter's gear. The whine of a crane moving into position. A dog whining in the distance. Perhaps a raven cawing and croaking. Of course, there were ravens on the mountainside, and a dead one within. But the more I listened, the more it sounded like a cry of some sort. Laughter, or tears? Was it a fox? Nakinngi?

I listened again, cupped my hands to my ears, and

then walked in the direction I presumed the sound to originate, retracing our steps back to the path. Another cry, but no closer. If anything, it was further away. I stopped and looked back at the cave beneath the boulder. I had already been gone longer than five minutes, and I was walking further away. If Maratse came out of the cave, and if I walked any further, he would not be able to see me. A thought flashed through my mind that I was being lured away from the policeman, that this was some grand design. I patted my pockets for the tupilaq, and realised that I had left it in the boat. I felt naked, all of a sudden, and an irrational fear began to gnaw at my stomach. I could still smell the tupilaq on my hands and I pressed them to my face.

"This is stupid," I said, aloud, keen to hear the sound of a human voice, something other than a cry on the wind.

I made a decision and turned back, moving quickly between the rocks and boulders, the edge of the ice on my left, as I headed back to the cave. Maratse was still lying down, as I squeezed between the rocks. I called his name and shook his shoulder, several times before he responded and opened one eye.

"What?" he said, his voice slurred and sleepy.

"I heard something. We have to go and look. Together."

"What did you hear?"

"I don't know. But I think we should investigate. We have come all this way," I said, and shook him again. "Maratse, we have to look."

It took a few minutes more before Maratse rolled onto his side and then crawled out of the cave. I followed and helped him to his feet once we were outside. The last light was waning, and the wind swirled a light breath of snow in beguiling blusters up and down the mountainside. Maratse wobbled for a second until he found his balance, and nodded that he was ready.

"It's this way," I said, and led him towards the path.

I grew confident at the sound of another cry on the wind, glancing at Maratse to see if he had heard it, but the policeman stumbled behind me, oblivious it seemed to anything other than the uneven surface between his feet. We reached the path, and I heard another cry and something louder, like the gnashing of two stones, or perhaps a slab of rock splitting as it fell onto another.

"We're close," I whispered, and then louder, "There. I see it."

PART 5

I held my breath at the sight of a small Arctic fox. It was a blue fox, the kind that did not change the colour of their fur from summer brown to winter white. The fox worried about the ice, keening in the wind, and I realised that I had been duped into thinking that it was Nakinngi's cries I had heard, the cry of a little boy lost, one that wanted to be found, and to be taken home to his mother. I steeled myself for Maratse's admonishment, but his silence was more worrying still. I turned to see him stagger to a boulder and sit down, shoulders hunched, his arms resting on his knees. He had pulled the wool hat as far down his brow as possible, and I saw him shiver, as I walked over to him.

"We have to get you back to the boat," I said. "I'm sorry I dragged you up here."

"It's a fox," Maratse said, lifting his finger to point at it. "A big one."

"It is a fox, but not very big."

"You're sure? It would make a good pelt. A lot of money."

"Perhaps. But it is small. A cub, looking for its mother maybe?"

"We should catch it." Maratse tried to stand. I pressed my hand on his shoulder but he slapped it away, waving for me to stand to one side as he lurched to his feet and fumbled for the pistol holstered on his belt.

"What are you doing?"

"I'm going to kill the fox." Maratse took a step forwards and tripped, one hand breaking his fall, the other gripping the butt of his pistol. He frowned, and looked up from the ground. "Help," he said. I helped him to his feet, and Maratse made another attempt at pulling his pistol free of the holster. The fox cub skittered back and forth on the ice in front of us.

"You should rest," I said, as I steadied Maratse. "Then we can walk back to the boat."

"The fox," he said. "It's so big."

"No, it's not. It's just a cub. Come on." I tried to pull Maratse back towards the boulder, but he shrugged out of my grip, whooping as he finally released the catch on the holster and waved the pistol in the air.

I had seen Maratse with a pistol in his hand before, had heard him fire it when we searched for Aqqalunnguaq. But here, at the edge of the ice sheet, Maratse was not well, he was armed, and we were a long way from home or help. I remembered his mobile, and pressed my hand on Maratse's arm.

"What?" he said.

"Your mobile. Let me call for help."

"What help? We're fine. Look," Maratse said and pointed at the fox with the barrel of his gun, "it's just sitting there. I will shoot it."

"No, Maratse. We have to go. You're sick."

Maratse pulled free of me for the second time, aimed at the fox, and fired. The report of the shot echoed around the mountain and the cub darted behind a boulder and out of sight. Maratse grunted, stumbled forwards and onto the ice. I followed him, my eyes on the gun wavering in his grip. Maratse slipped, cursing as his knee crunched onto the surface. He pressed the barrel of the pistol into the ice, leaned against it, and stood up.

"Did you see it?" he said.

"Yes, but…"

"Where?"

"Over there, behind the boulder."

Maratse wobbled again, and then walked towards the boulder. I followed, just a few steps behind him, wondering if we would be hurt or killed from the ricochet of a bullet if he fired his gun at the rocks.

I heard another sound, too loud to be the fox moving about on the rocks, but not a cry. It was the sound of small stones shifting and scraping as something large moved. Maratse saw it before me, and he shushed me with a finger, as I stood beside him. He pointed, and I followed the tip of his finger to a boulder trapped in the ice and a pair of eyes peeping over it.

"*Erqigdlit*," Maratse whispered, grinning, as he pointed the pistol.

"No," I said, and walked in front of him, "it's the boy." I turned my back on Maratse and waved at the boy behind the boulder. Even in the gloom his black hair shone, a stark contrast to the white of the ice. I saw the boy's hands, the colour of hazelnuts, as he placed his fingers in front of his face and rested his chin on his thumbs. "It's all right," I said. "We've come to help you."

There was a sparkle in the boy's eyes, and I felt a rush of elation as I realised we had found him. He was exactly where the shaman had said he would be. And, as far as I could tell, he was unharmed. I waved for him to come out from behind the boulder, and he nodded. His head bobbed out of sight, and when he stepped into view and onto the ice, I saw that he carried something in his hands. It was a large blue fox, almost as long as the boy was tall. The back legs dangled down in front of the boy's, as he held it under its forelegs, the head and muzzle dipping down, and lost in the shadows of the evening and the blue fleece the boy wore. The fox's tail dangled between the boy's legs, twisting as he walked towards me.

"Hey," Maratse called out. I turned around and saw Maratse point the pistol at the boy. "Watch out," he said.

"What's wrong? It's the boy. It's Nakinngi."

"No, Maratse said, "it is the *erqigdlit*." He cupped one hand beneath the other, and steadied his aim.

"Stop, Maratse," I said, and waved my hands. "It is the boy." I glanced over my shoulder as Nakinngi stopped, as if his feet were frozen to the ice. He stared at the gun in Maratse's hand, and then darted across the ice, away from the boulder, further up the mountainside, the tail of the fox bouncing with each step. Maratse tracked him with the pistol. "No," I shouted, as he pulled the trigger.

The second report of the gun was louder than the first. I twisted to see Nakinngi tumble to the ground, and took a step towards him. But Maratse was still aiming, and I was torn between checking the boy, and stopping the man. I took two steps towards Maratse, lunged for the gun in his hand, and we tumbled to the ground. The pistol slid across the ice and splashed into a stream of melt water. He slapped at my arms as I wrestled him to the ice, and then he was still, lying on his side, panting, sweating, and shivering. I waited until his eyes were open, and then stood up.

"I'm going to check on the boy," I said. "Stay here."

I picked up the pistol first, shaking the water out of the barrel, and stuffing it into the pocket of my overalls. Then I looked to where I had seen Nakinngi fall, only to realise he was gone. I called his name, and started to jog up the slope, avoiding the smooth ice where possible. The surface was pocked with blackheads, small stones warmed by the sun and melted to within a centimetre of the surface. I slid across them, catching my breath at the sight of a body on the ice. It was the fox; Nakinngi must have left it when Maratse opened fire.

It occurred to me that the boy might not understand Danish, but I called his name again, and again, until he lifted his head from where he lay on the ice, some twenty metres from the fox. He had not gone far from his prize, and I could feel his gaze as I stooped to pick up the fox and stroke the soft fur. The body was still warm, the nose bloody. I held out the fox and the boy stood up. He started walking towards me, veering to one side to look at Maratse.

"It's okay," I said. "He won't shoot at you again." I smiled, waited for the boy to come closer, and said, "Are you hurt?"

The boy shook his head.

"This is yours," I said, and pressed the fox into his arms, as he came closer. The boy smiled, and I pointed at the blood coming out of the fox's nose. "How did you kill it?"

The boy said something very fast in Greenlandic, pausing once or twice as I frowned. He tucked the fox under one arm, and pointed with the other, gesturing for me to follow him back to the boulder. We both looked at Maratse as we walked.

"I'm just going to see something," I called out, as we passed. "I'll be with you in just a moment."

The boy led me behind the boulder and showed

me a trap he had built with rocks. There was a scattering of food beneath a large slab of stone. The boy talked as he demonstrated how he positioned the stone above two flat supporting pieces of rock, one of which sat on a trigger of wood. The food was scattered on the trigger, and the weight of the fox sprang the trap, releasing the heavy stone on top of its head. The boy was clearly proud of what he had built, and stroked the head of the fox.

"Smart," I said, and smiled. "Is your name Nakinngi?"

"*Iji*," he said.

"Nakinngi, we have come to take you home. Do you understand?"

The boy nodded, and said something in Greenlandic, the same dialect as Maratse.

"Okay," I said. "But first we have to help my friend, the policeman. He is not well."

Nakinngi frowned and clutched the fox closer to his body.

"He doesn't want your fox," I said, and then wondered how I would explain what it was that Maratse thought he had seen when he shot at the boy. That thought made me wonder about the tupilaq, and just how Ivik had intended for it to protect us. Of course, the tupilaq was still in Maratse's dinghy. "Perhaps that's why it all went so wrong," I whispered. Nakinngi frowned, and I said, "It's all right; I'm just talking to myself."

I heard a small cry behind us, and turned to see the fox cub standing on a rock a little further up the mountainside than the boulder. It was going to have to fend for itself now, and I wondered if it had learned enough from its mother to survive the winter.

The boy stood up and I followed him back across the ice to Maratse.

Nakinngi stopped a short distance from the policeman. I whispered that it was okay, as I walked past to kneel on the ice beside Maratse. I pressed my hand on Maratse's shoulder, and then tugged off my glove to place my palm on his brow. His skin was hot to the touch, and yet his body shivered. I wondered if it was because of the ice, or the fever.

"We have to move him," I said to Nakinngi. "Come, you must help me."

There was no way we were going to get Maratse down to the boat, but he needed some kind of shelter, we all did, if we were going to survive the night on the mountainside. I wondered how long Nakinngi had been here, where he had slept, and what he had eaten, and then I remembered the cave.

"Maratse," I said. "You have to get up. We're going to get you back to the cave. Then you can sleep. I promise."

Maratse opened his eyes. He blinked and looked at me, looked at Nakinngi, and then he looked at the fox.

PART 6

If ever I had doubted that Maratse was sick, his ramblings in Danish, as we stumbled to the cave, confirmed it. The man was heavy with fever. His gaze flickered from the path to the boy to the fox. Always the fox. I thought about what the shaman had said about the *erqigdlit*, or, rather, what he had not said. He had praised the beasts while sewing the limbs to the tupilaq, and I wondered if Maratse's fever was in some way the personification of the beasts. The environment, our surroundings, made it easy to expand upon the weird and wonderful, to believe in myths, to be susceptible to monsters.

"The tupilaq is for protection," Ivik had said. "Keep it with you."

We stopped to let Maratse rest for a moment. Nakinngi hid behind my legs, fearful, perhaps, of Maratse's intentions. His focus was on the fox, and I recalled the image of Maratse sitting at the kitchen table, as the shaman spun the myth story, sewed the tupilaq, and teased the policeman. Was there something darker at play, I wondered. Were we the subject of some black magic, Arctic voodoo or the like? Did I not pay enough, or had the shaman expected more? A tip of some kind.

The rational part of my brain took over. We had the found the boy. Against all the odds, he was exactly where the shaman had said he would be. This was something that made me wonder, again, at the shaman's role in this adventure. But Maratse's fever had begun in Tasiilaq, his colleague had said as much. So he was not cursed, he simply had a cold – a cold that had developed into a raging fever, most likely the product of sailing across the fjord and climbing the mountain. Maratse's fascination with the fox and the transformation of the boy holding it into some mythical beast was a feverish interpretation of what Maratse could see, and it would disappear with his fever. He needed to rest, he needed shelter, and he needed some kind of medication.

"Maratse," I said, "do you have a first aid kit on the boat?" He grunted something, and tried to stand. I pressed him back onto the boulder, and said, "Pills of some kind. Headache pills? Aspirin?"

"*Iji*," he said.

"Good." I helped him to his feet and we walked the last ten metres to the cave.

Maratse seemed to understand that if he crawled between the rocks he could lie down. I let him go first, wondering what he could use as a pillow, until I noticed that he crawled into exactly the same position he had found before, his head on a smooth rock, and his back in a shallow depression between the rocks. I was struck with the thought that he was not the first to lie inside this cave. The boy stayed outside, the fox clutched to his chest.

"I am going back to the boat," I said, placing my hand on Maratse's chest. "Try and rest. I'll be back as soon as I can." I felt the familiar shape of Maratse's mobile, and tugged it out of his pocket, only to return it when I realised that the battery was dead. I listened to Maratse, as he began to snore, and then backed out of the cave to join the boy.

Nakinngi watched me as I stood up, flicking his gaze to the cave and entrance and me. He pointed at the cave and said something in Greenlandic.

"It's all right," I said, "he is sleeping. But we need

to go to the boat, to see if there is any medicine for him. Do you understand?"

"*Iji*," Nakinngi said. He stood up, tucked the fox beneath his arm, and started walking towards the path.

"Don't you want to leave that behind?" I asked, pointing at the fox.

"*Eeqqi*," he said, with a glance at Maratse, and another at the sky. I thought about the raven, and other predators on the mountainside. And then I thought of food, and the fact that we didn't have any.

"Nakinngi," I said, "where did you sleep?"

He pointed into the distance, beyond the path, and beyond the boulder where he had built his stone trap.

"And do you have any food?"

He shrugged, pinched the air between his finger and thumb, and said, "A little."

"You do speak Danish," I said, and smiled. Nakinngi pinched the air again, and grinned.

I stumbled over a rock and stopped to catch my balance. When I lifted my head, I felt a rush of blood pumping at my temples. Nakinngi watched me, his small brow furrowed, and I felt his sympathy lift me, and I straightened my back.

"It's all right," I said. "I'm just a bit tired."

Nakinngi did not seem convinced. He led me past the boulder with the trap, and into his camp. I heard the familiar flap and snap of a plastic tarpaulin before I saw it, stretched as it was low over the ground. To my European eyes, the young hunter had constructed a perfect replication of a lean-to, just high enough from the ground for him to crawl inside. The ground beneath the tarpaulin was ordered with squares of rocks like drawers for his equipment – a tin opener beside a tin of ravioli, a broad knife with a plastic handle inside a plastic sheath. There was a bottle of water and a plastic cup, but little else, and no extra clothing. It seemed that Nakinngi was wearing everything he possessed, and I wondered why he was not colder than he was. The rim of the tin of ravioli was pitted. Flakes of rust crumbled into my skin as I picked it up. I looked at the water in the bottle, and decided to leave it, taking the cup instead, and pocketing the tin opener. Nakinngi nodded his approval as I squeezed the tin inside the large thigh pocket of my overalls. He reached out as I began to wobble at the effort of pocketing the tin, and I leaned against the boulder for a second, before regaining my balance. I wiped my nose, the hairs in my nostrils prickling at another whiff of tupilaq.

"Thank you," I said. I pointed in the direction of the path, and Nakinngi led the way. The tarpaulin flapped again, and I took one last look at the boy's camp, impressed once more at the skills of the young hunter.

The thought lingered for a moment, but then I found I needed to concentrate as the light faded and the path became increasingly difficult to navigate. I slipped on loose scree, stumbled over the rocks, and bumped my knees against shadow boulders more than once. Nakinngi seemed to dance in front of me, the tail of the fox bouncing just above the small of his back, as he carried it under one arm. I caught a chuckle in my throat at how uncanny it was that the shaman should talk of the *erqigdlit* when I had a living specimen right in front of me – a boy with a fox' tail. And then the boat was in sight, and the path levelled out, and I practically ran the last few metres.

Nakinngi leaned over the side of Maratse's dinghy and pointed at his backpack. I lifted it out of the boat and handed it to him.

"*Eeqqi*," he said, and shook his head.

"You don't want it?"

Nakinngi shrugged and lifted the fox in his arms. I nodded and placed his pack back in the boat. Nakinngi didn't look once at the broken hull of the dinghy beside Maratse's. Not even when I pointed at it and asked if it was his. He said nothing.

"But you came in that boat, didn't you?"

Nakinngi shrugged and pointed up the mountain, to the right of the path, in the direction of the cave. I looked up at the dark grey clouds, and the shadows creeping along the path. He was right, we should be going. We could talk more in the cave.

I climbed into Maratse's boat and began my search for a first aid kit. There was nothing in the watertight chest in which he had stored our overalls, and after a few minutes I began to give up hope of ever finding it, wondering if there even was such a kit on board. I lifted the dirty cloth containing the tupilaq, and found a small red bag tucked inside a compartment in the seat. I tucked the tupilaq under my arm and unzipped the bag. Hidden between a couple of plasters and a single triangular bandage was a plastic Ziploc bag containing a strip of tablets. I turned the strip between my fingers and read the lettering printed on the top. It was aspirin, eight tablets in all. I pocketed the tablets, and then stuffed the first aid kit in another pocket. I put the tupilaq on the centre seat as I searched for and found Maratse's satchel containing a thermos of coffee and a packet of biscuits. I slipped it over my shoulder.

"Ready," I said, and smiled at Nakinngi. I looked up the path, and waited as another wave of dizziness washed over me. I took a deep breath, and nodded for Nakinngi to lead the way.

I felt something tugging at my conscience as I took a step away from the boat. When I turned, the first thing I noticed was the tupilaq, bound as it was inside the dirty cloth. It occurred to me that the tupilaq had led me to the tablets, and I wondered if that was mere coincidence. I allowed myself the luxury of pretending that it was more than that. I had paid for protection, and, for five hundred kroner, I could be convinced that the tupilaq was doing what I had been told it would. I opened Maratse's satchel, and stuffed the tupilaq inside, wrinkling my nose at the bubble of air I pressed out of the bindings.

"It can't hurt to bring it with me," I said, and waved to Nakinngi that I was coming.

The climb to the cave took longer than I imagined, and it wasn't just the long shadows at my feet and failing light above that slowed me down. I stopped in between to catch my breath and to stop my head from spinning. I was hot, but as soon as I unzipped the front of my overalls, I began to shiver, and zipped them back up again. Nakinngi bounded in front of me, his tail bouncing with each step. I envied his youth, his energy, and I appreciated the furrow of worry he wore on his brow when he stopped and waited for me.

"I'm all right," I said, when I paused beside him. "Just tired. It has been a long day. But we found you."

Nakinngi smiled. He took another step, and then a bound, and for a moment, I was sure I saw him scrabble with feet and hands together, though how he didn't drop the fox I could not say.

He led me all the way to the cave, waited as I crawled between the rocks, and stooped at the entrance, watching as I roused Maratse to give him two tablets, and a sip of cold coffee. I pressed a biscuit into Maratse's hand, and turned to offer the packet to Nakinngi. The boy shook his head.

"All right," I said, and then, "Won't you come inside?"

He shook his head again, and moved just out of sight. I let him go, listened to the sound of Maratse breathing deeply, and decided that it couldn't hurt to rest. Just for a moment. I pulled the tin of ravioli from my pocket, and decided that it would be just as good for breakfast, as it would be for dinner. It could wait, I thought. I used Maratse's satchel for a pillow, and lay down beside him.

PART 7

My fever dream answered no questions, and I had plenty as I lay inside the cave, sweating and shivering. Whatever protection the tupilaq afforded, I did not care, as my focus was on the strange beasts, half-human, half-wolf, like lupine centaurs, grooming and resting on the ice, above the rock, below the summit of the mountain. One beast in particular caught my mind's eye. I couldn't say if she was the alpha female, but the males doted on her, and I understood why, as she fixed her large brown eyes on me, and the men teased the knots and tangles from her long black hair. It reached down the length of her creamy torso, hid her naked breasts, and shone in the moonlight. I don't remember having seen a night sky so clear in all the time I lived in Greenland. It was as if the stars themselves were in awe of the woman's beauty. And yet, the beast grew from the waist down. She had no navel, not that I could see, hidden as it was beneath the layer of fur, white fur, the fur of the Arctic wolf. She tipped her head to one side, staring at me, as the male on her right used his teeth to remove a stubborn knot of hair. When he was finished, the female lay down, curling her hind legs beneath her, swishing her tail, and resting her chin on her arms folded on the ground in front of her.

She was captivating. I was captivated. There, on the ice, the beast, and yes, such beauty.

I must have murmured or groaned in my sleep, as the next thing I remembered was Maratse shaking me awake, and the *erqigdlit* were gone.

"Eat," he said, as I opened my eyes. He pressed a biscuit into my hand and poured a cup of coffee, cold, just like I had served him. "Take these." He pressed two tablets into the palm of my hand.

I swallowed the tablets and looked around the cave. It was lighter than before, we must have slept through the night. I leaned forwards to peer through the entrance.

"What are you looking for?" Maratse asked, as he pressed me gently back onto the ground.

"Not what, but who. Where is the boy?"

"The boy?"

"Nakinngi. The boy we have been searching for. The one we found yesterday."

Maratse nodded, screwed the lid onto the thermos, and tapped a cigarette out of the packet from his jacket pocket. "The boy," he said, and stuck the cigarette between the gap in his teeth. He played with the lighter in his hand, and said, "When you are well enough, I will show you."

"I'm well now," I said, anxious to see Nakinngi.

"Rest a bit longer. I will be back in an hour." Maratse crawled out of the cave. I caught a whiff of smoke as he lit his cigarette. I listened to the tramp of his boots on the rock as he walked away from the cave, and then I was alone.

I lay down and waited for the girl to return, as I searched for her between the boundary of ice and rock. Maratse's comment about the boy made me wonder what else I had imagined during our search. I put it out of my mind. He would wake me in an hour, and, for the moment at least, I needed to rest.

Maratse shook me awake, and waited as I zipped the front of my overalls. He gathered our belongings, stuffed them inside his satchel, and then gestured at the entrance. I waved that I was ready. My legs trembled a little as I stood up and took my first breath of cool air on the second day of our search.

"Over here," Maratse said, and led me towards the path. He waited as I found my feet, and then we stepped onto the ice. I slipped once, shaking the image of the *erqigdlit* from my mind as I pushed myself to my feet. Maratse gripped my arm and helped me stand. "There, behind the boulder," he said.

I followed him across the ice to the spot where Nakinngi had shown me his stone fox trap. It looked older than I remembered. The wooden trigger was grey and fibrous, the crumbs were gone, and there was no fox, just a scattering of bones picked clean by ravens.

"You talked in your sleep," Maratse said. "Something about a trap. I found it."

"Nakinngi showed it to me," I said. "He was very proud of it."

"No," Maratse said, and shook his head. He slipped another cigarette between his teeth and lit it. "Come. There's more."

Maratse led me further from the path and I heard a snap of plastic. It must have been from Nakinngi's camp, but the tarpaulin Maratse showed me looked like a thin string vest stretched taut between the rocks. It would have given the boy no protection at all, not from the wind, the sun, the snow, the rain – nothing. Maratse took the tin of ravioli from the satchel and showed me the best before date.

"March," I said.

"*Iiji*, nineteen ninety-two." Maratse caught my eye, and said, "Twenty-three years ago." He put the tin on the ground inside the square of rocks, together with the tin opener."

"You're putting it back?"

He shrugged. "Like a museum."

I looked at the bottle of water, and remembered not wanting to take it the night before, and little wonder, it was uncapped, the contents grey and course with silt.

"Nakinngi didn't camp here, did he?"

"*Eeqqi*," Maratse said. He lit his cigarette and started walking towards the path. "I was up early," he said. He patted the holster on his belt, and said, "I found my pistol in your pocket. I'm sorry about that."

"It's all right," I said. "You weren't well."

"What do you remember?" Maratse walked by my side as we started down the path. The rocks were slippery and we took our time, two fever-ridden men forced to spend a night on the mountain.

"I remember finding the boy, and you shooting at him."

"Hmm."

"You missed," I said, and then, "but he wasn't there. Was he?"

We walked a little further until we could see the boats on the beach below, and Maratse said, "I didn't see a boy. I was shooting at something else." He looked away for a moment. "Ivik filled my head with beasts. I wasn't well. I'm sorry."

"There's no need to be sorry. I knew you weren't well, but what about me. I saw Nakinngi. But," I said, as Maratse shook his head, "I didn't think I had your fever."

"You didn't." He opened the satchel and pulled out the tupilaq. The hairs in my nose twitched at the smell reeking out of the bindings, as Maratse undid them. "Ivik charged the tupilaq with magic, but not like they did in the old days. He used something else."

Maratse placed the tupilaq on the ground and opened the cloth, peeling it back like a shroud. The effigy inside was almost putrid, the sinews thin and eroded, the rubber-rotten flesh was soft, and the stomach had stained the cloth black.

"Old tupilaq were charged with the shaman's semen," Maratse said, "to give them power. Ivik charged this with something else. A chemical." He picked up a thin twig from the coarse bush growing among the Arctic grasses, and poked the tupilaq in the torso. "Whatever he used has evaporated, but you had the tupilaq next to you the whole time in the boat."

"You're saying I was hallucinating?"

"*Iji.*"

"Then what about the boy?"

Maratse tossed the twig to one side, wrapped the cloth around the tupilaq and stuffed it into his satchel. "This way," he said, and continued down the path to the boats.

I waited, as Maratse dumped his satchel onto the centre seat. He flicked the butt of his cigarette onto the beach, and pointed at the hull of the boat.

"The boat is old, but not the damage. This," he said, and bent down on one knee, "is where it hit something."

"What?"

"I don't know. Maybe a pallet from the docks?"

"A pallet?"

"They lie flat in the water," he said, and held his palm flat between us, "just below the surface. From a distance they are invisible. If a boat hits it at speed it will sink it." He stood up. "It has happened before."

"And you think that happened to Nakinngi?"

"Maybe." Maratse waved for me to follow him.

We walked to the west of the beach, following the coast, across rocks, and then down onto small pebble beaches encrusted with ornaments of ice. The beaches were the colour of burnt toast, the ice white, sometimes blue depending upon the light and the age of the water frozen within it. The grasses were a mix of greens and straws. All natural colours. The shock of bright blue clinging to the next beach was out of place, and I knew at once that it was Nakinngi.

Maratse was the first to step on the beach. He stopped me with a flat palm on my chest.

"He has been here a few days," he said.

"Yes," I said, and looked around Maratse's shoulder.

"Ravens have picked at his body. Maybe you shouldn't look."

"I want to see him."

"Hmm." Maratse tapped my chest and stepped back. "Okay." He led the way.

Nakinngi's fingers were white and wrinkled. They clutched the sand, his small nails buried to the quick. His face, hidden by his hood, looked in the opposite direction to where we stood. I took a step to go around his body, to see his face. I was curious to discover if it was the same boy I had imagined on the ice. I had never seen a photo of Nakinngi, and only met his father once. Perhaps, he looked like his mother? But I had only seen her sob, and his sisters' faces had been hidden by long dark hair.

"You're sure?" Maratse said, as I walked around Nakinngi.

I hesitated. Convinced that I was, but still, not sure. Not sure at all. I crouched by Nakinngi's face, and reached out, ready to peel back his hood, as Maratse had peeled back the shroud of the tupilaq. I hesitated once more, the cold, wet rim of the boy's hood, sticky between my fingers.

"What was he doing out here?" I asked, the hood trembling within my grasp.

Maratse lit another cigarette. "He came here to be a man," he said. "Like his father. There are foxes all over Greenland, but this mountain," Maratse said, and nodded at the summit, "is known for its blue foxes. Their pelts are good now. They are nice and fat. Shiny. Just before the winter. Nakinngi came here because he listened to stories from old hunters. I think the boat belongs to his grandfather. I have to tell him that his grandson died on a hunting trip." Maratse puffed a cloud of smoke above his head.

"And what about Ivik? How did he know to come here? Could he have killed the boy?"

"Ivik saw the boat, or maybe heard about it. He didn't kill the boy." Maratse glanced in the direction of his dinghy. "But, I can get your money back. Charge him with poisoning you."

"No," I said. "Let him keep his money."

The hood grew heavy between my fingers, but I was ready. I could feel it. Soon we would carry the boy back to Maratse's dinghy, to return him to his father, and then his mother, his sisters, his grandfather. But before then, in the next few moments, I needed to know, to see if this Nakinngi was *my* Nakinngi, to see if the boy in the sand was the boy on the ice.

I peeled back the hood.

And on that beach, in the fjord, above the roots of the mountain, embraced by the cold whisper of the icebergs, I discovered that I believed in magic.

AUTHOR'S NOTE

The mountain on the cover is on the island of Uummannaq, on the west coast of Greenland. In the summer of 2010, just a few days prior to starting a month-long solo kayak expedition in the area, I checked in with the local police. After approving my safety plan, one of the senior officers asked me to keep an eye out for the bodies of three young men. They had gone missing a day earlier when their boat hit a wooden pallet floating in the water.

Their bodies were never found.

Chris
January 2018
Denmark

ARCTIC SHORTS

The *Arctic Shorts*, of which *Katabatic* is the first short story, introduce the character of Police Constable David Maratse, a Greenlander from Ittoqqortoormiit on the east coast.

Maratse first appeared in *The Ice Star*, and the sequel *In the Shadow of the Mountain*, alongside Konstabel Fenna Brongaard of the Sirius Sledge Patrol. These stories are set prior to those events. However, Maratse will return in his own series of crime novels, set in Greenland, in the new year. His own stand-alone series will be set after the events of *The Ice Star* and its sequels.

The Arctic Shorts series includes:
KATABATIC (story one)
CONTAINER (story two)
TUPILAQ (story three)

The Greenland Trilogy includes:
THE ICE STAR (book one)
IN THE SHADOW OF THE MOUNTAIN
(book two)
THE SHAMAN'S HOUSE (book three)

Katabatic is written in British English and makes use of several Danish and Greenlandic words.

A GREENLANDIC GLOSSARY

Police Constable David Maratse is from the east coast of Greenland. East Greenlandic is a dialect of Greenlandic. There is, to date, no real written record of the language and children in East Greenland are required to learn West Greenlandic. For Maratse to learn English, he would have had to learn West Greenlandic, then Danish and English as his fourth language. There are no foreign language dictionaries translating East Greenlandic words to English. English is predominantly taught through Danish, with all explanations and points of grammar written in Danish. Many East Greenlanders learn English, but it is far from easy.

Here is a very brief glossary of the few East Greenlandic words used in *Katabatic*, and the English equivalents.

<u>East Greenlandic/English</u>
iiji / yes
eeqqi / no*
qujanaq/qujanaraali / thank you
iserniaa / come in
*Naamik (West Greenlandic) / no

ABOUT THE AUTHOR

Christoffer Petersen is the author's pen name. Chris lived in Greenland for seven years, and continues to be inspired by the vast icy wilderness of the Arctic. His books share a common setting in the Arctic region, often with a Scandinavian influence.

You can find Chris in Denmark or online here:

www.christoffer-petersen.com

BY THE SAME AUTHOR

THE GREENLAND TRILOGY
featuring Konstabel Fenna Brongaard

THE ICE STAR (book one)
IN THE SHADOW OF THE MOUNTAIN
(book two)
THE SHAMAN'S HOUSE (book three)

THE CANADIAN QUARTET (2018)
featuring Konstabel Fenna Brongaard

BLOOD SPOOR (book one)

GREENLAND CRIME (2018)
featuring Constable David Maratse

SEVEN GRAVES, ONE WINTER (book one)

ARCTIC SHORTS
featuring Constable David Maratse

KATABATIC (story one)
CONTAINER (story two)
TUPILAQ (story three)
THE LAST FLIGHT (story four)

Printed in Great Britain
by Amazon